THE RANCHER'S DAUGHTER

2

Dedication

The Author would like to dedicate the book to her husband who she has been married to for 55 years.

She would like to thank him for his full support.

His name is John.

Acknowledgments

Thankyou for all your support Vivian.

About the Author

I am a 75 year old lady who loves to read books. I have always dreamed of writing a book and having it published. I have been happily married to my husband of 55 years and raised 2 lovely children, whom I am so proud of. I have always lived in a beautiful part of the United Kingdom the Eden Valley. Growing up was hard but with hard work together with my husband and children built a successful business. I am an old romantic and I hope you enjoy this story as much as I have enjoyed writing it.

Table of Contents

Chapter 1

Jack was standing at the kitchen window, and he turned to Norma, his wife.

"I am watching Alisha out there with the horses. She has something special with animals. They have an affinity with her, she will be an excellent trainer one day."

Ma turned to Pa and replied.

"She has schooling to get through, and then she can make her choice then." "Always a big life's choice. I am sure she will be up to making the right choice when the time comes."

"Ma, come and watch her mount Charlie, her pony, she has good skills at keeping her horse steady as she mounts her long legs. Only 10 years old, and her body is in a perfect stance, a joy to watch."

In the distance, Alisha was also being watched by the ranch hand Daniel West. Daniel was 20 years of age, and he also saw potential in the young girl. He was a rodeo rider in his spare time and competed in lots of events. He enjoyed the rewards when he won, not just the financial rewards but the attention from the ladies he attracted. No one was special in his love life, and he was in no rush for anything serious.

Alisha rode her pony out and then returned to the stable, where she dismounted and unsaddled Charlie. She started to groom him, chatting as she did, smoothing his coat to a soft glean. Alisha could see in the corner of her eyes that someone was present and turned around to see Daniel, the ranch hand mounting his horse with strength and agility.

Ranching and animals were always Alisha's love, and after leaving school, she enrolled in a veterinary college in Denver for 4 years. She returned home whenever she could. She adjusted to life as a student well, and she had the capability to make friends and socialise easily. She dabbled in a couple of romantic relationships, with on-off relations with fellow students, and found that sex was not all that it was cracked up to be. She managed to keep her heart intact.

Alisha eventually graduated as a fully pledged veterinary doctor.

Before taking up a full-time job, she decided to return home and chill out for a while. She took on jobs on the ranch, also helping Ma in the house. When it came to the roundup of the herd, she jumped at the challenge of long days on horseback, which was rough work on hard, dusty plains. Daniel didn't seem too pleased to have her with the crew and tried to keep an eye on her so as not to get in any danger. Pa and Ma would have his hide if anything were to happen to their beloved daughter. Rounding the herd is a two-day job, and towards the end of the first day, when the cattle lay to rest, wagons were checked and tied up, and supper was prepared. Alisha was extremely hot and dirty and made comments around the camp that she would take herself to the river and get a wash. Daniel heard of her plans "you must not go off on your own."

Alisha looked at him displeased and was not happy at his comment.

"I am quite used to looking after myself."

Daniel was agitated.

"In no uncertain terms, as long as I am in charge, you don't go alone, you will go with an escort" "I know where you can get a lovely shower in clear waters." Daniel had visited there many times before.

"Saddle up, young lady, before it gets dark."

Reluctantly Alisha turned her back on Dan and gathered her toiletries up, and strode over to where her horse was tethered. Dan was already waiting for her.

"Do you want a hand to mount up?"

Alisha replied sharply, "I'll manage. Thank you."

They rode out of camp with the other hands watching closely. They were mocking each other and digging each in the ribs. Alisha, as she rode, started to consider if she would be granted privacy to undress and shower, she had no intention of giving a strip show.

The river came into view about half a mile along the track. Daniel obviously knew where he needed to be, and eventually, they came to an area where the river was overlooked by rocks, and the river ran over an area. "Make yourself ready while I tie the horses."

Alisha was pleased. "Oh, that's good of you." Alisha got her rolled-up towel off the back of her horse, looked for a place she felt safe, and went ahead to remove her clothes. She very carefully went to the edge of the river where the waterfall was cascading down. She stepped into the water, which was very cool and exhilarating. Suddenly two arms came from behind her and pulled her into another body.

"Don't panic," Dan said.

"I am just making sure you don't slip, just lean into me, and we can get a beautiful shower with no one in any difficulties."

Alisha was startled.

"Crikey, you have done this deliberately."

Dan laughed.

"I didn't, but I sure am pleased I decided to come and hold you in case you slipped – you do feel mighty wonderful."

Dan then smacked Alisha on her bum and turned her around to face him.

Alisha shrieked, "what do you think you are doing?"

"I know what I would like to do, but don't worry, you're safe with me. It's been a pleasure. I won't forget in a hurry. Now come on, I'll help you get dry, and you can get your clothes on."

Shocked, Alisha replied.

"I can dry myself, thank you."

A smirking Dan "Oh come on, don't be a spoilsport. Would you like to share my sleeping bag tonight?"

"NO, get lost."

"Funny, I thought that's what you would say. Never mind, nice memories."

Alisha dried herself and dressed, feeling refreshed but was narked. She had always had an eye on Daniel, but she was too young for him. They rode back to the camp in silence.

The camp was quiet, and the men were sat chatting.

Dan asked, "are the cattle settled?"

"Yep, all is ok."

The sleeping bag felt cold in the night, and Alisha wondered what it would have been like if Daniel had shared it with her. Pondering what if those thoughts kept her awake until the sun rose. A tired Alisha got up, dressed, ate a bacon bun, and had several cups of coffee. By this time, the cattle were starting to move, and they started the rest of the journey home.

Chapter 2

Ma and Pa welcomed her home and overwhelmed her with questions about the trip. She gave her report but didn't mention her shared shower. Alisha spent a leisurely day after her long ride on the round-up. Aching legs, she helped her Ma to do some cooking. Around 3 pm, Daniel knocked at the door before entering and made his way to speak to Alisha.

"I wonder if you could give me your help? My horse has decided to go into giving birth, and she is having difficulty. I could do with your expertise."

Alisha was pleased she had been asked.

"No problem, I'll put on a boilersuit. I will come to the stable in a few minutes."

When Alisha entered the stable, she found Daniel talking and trying to soothe his horse, Ruby. Alisha put her bag down with all her equipment in and took out long rubber gloves and a tube of oil. She coated her hands with the oil. She stood at the back of Ruby and went ahead to enter the horse's birthing channel. Her hands were smaller than a man's and made entry easier. Alisha gauged that the foal was coming out with a leg at the wrong angle, with a few adjustments, she put a rope around its legs and started to pull. Ruby was tired and obviously had enough. Daniel stroked and soothed her as best he could, and with another heave, out came a beautiful colt. Ruby turned with the help of Dan, who was like a proud father and started to lick her newborn foal.

Alisha checked everything was in order and cleaned up the area around them. Within an hour, the colt stood up and was encouraged to bond with Ruby right away.

"How can I thank you?"

An incredibly happy Dan took hold of Alisha's arms.

"I must give you some money, and I must pay you."

Alisha replied.

"Not at all. It was just a good practice for me."

"Let me take you out for dinner Saturday night? I will be on maternity duty tonight."

"We can't, Saturday. It's the barbecue after the round-up."

 A barbecue and dance always prevailed over a round-up.

"Right, well, another night," said Dan.

"I will hold you to that, Dan."

"Once again, a very grateful thanks you were amazing."

Saturday arrived, and the ranch hands made ready for the barbeque and dance. Firewood was collected for the bonfire, as was the stage built for the band and a clearing made for dancing. Ma had been busy with Alisha most of the day preparing food to cook at the barbecue. Ma oversaw the barbecue and cooked steaks, chicken, and corn. Ladies had prepared sweets, and a bar was provided with drinks of all kinds. It was busy, and Alisha helped Ma and Pa to serve food and clear plates. A dance followed the lovely food, and those who weren't too full took to the dance floor with their partners, dancing to country-style music.

Alisha noticed Daniel sitting on a high stool at the bar with a pint of beer. He was dressed in black jeans, a white shirt, and a black jacket – Alisha thought he was very eye-catching. Alisha herself was dressed in a multi-colored skirt that came down to her calves, and she wore ankle boots. Her top was black and low revealing. She thought it was presentable for kicking up her heels. Many men asked her to dance and maybe wanted a bit more. Dan watched her every move, and when the music took on a smoochy tone, he made his move.

Alisha felt a tap on her shoulder, and Dan was standing there

"Our turn to dance would you do me the honour?" said Dan.

Alisha could feel herself blushing but held out her hand to be led to the dance floor. They pulled in close, and

Dan felt his body responding to Alisha's closeness and started to feel a connection. A connection that had been increasing recently. The music ended, and it was time to clear up. Dan thanked Alisha for their dance, and Alisha placed a quick kiss on his cheek and said goodnight. They both went about clearing up.

After tidying up, Alisha walked towards home but, on passing the stables, decided to look at Dan's new foal. Alisha entered the stable and looked over the railing, and mother and colt looked to be doing just fine. Alisha heard someone enter the stable and turned to see Daniel.

 "I saw the light on in the stable, and I thought it would be you, Alisha."

Daniel headed over and patted the new colt and an immensely proud mother. Daniel turned to Alisha.

"They both seem fine. Would you like to come to my bunkhouse for a coffee?"

Alisha replied.

 "I was going to make one when I got in, so that would be grand."

Dan gave a bit of fresh hay to the horses, took hold of Alisha's hand, and guided her into his bunkhouse. Alisha's heart was beating fast. She had never been in it before and looked around and noticed it was sparsely furnished but neat and clean. Dan made two cups of coffee and handed one to Alisha.

"Sit down and make yourself comfortable you must be ready for a rest?"

"I can't argue with that" Alisha proceeded to sit down.

Dan asked.

"Is it all right if I sit beside you? Cause if it is, I won't bite."

Alisha grinned

"Oh, that's a pity. I am sure I would like it."

She blushed on saying this.

"Daniel, I have to say, "I know I am a lot younger than you, but you have always had a special place in my heart. I missed seeing you when I was away at college. I have those memories of you swinging your legs over your horse's back – it gave me goosebumps."

Daniel smiled, his eyes sparkling. "Well, let me tell you, Alisha, I dare not look at you too much because of our age difference. If your Pa had been aware of my feelings for you, I would have been on the next horse out of here."

This excited Alisha "and how do you feel now, Dan?"

"Alisha, I dare not think about how I feel about you. I am just a ranch hand with no home of my own and 10 years older than you. That's not a good start."

"Dan, I don't care about any of those things. I just feel a strong bond towards you."

"Alisha, can I hold you in my arms and perhaps kiss you?"

"Please, Dan, I would like to give that a try."

Daniel pulled Alisha closer. "Come here. I promised myself this would never happen."

"Well, it is going to, and we have to give it a try. We need to know."

Daniel spoke softly.

"I know now, without trying, I am seriously attracted to you, Alisha."

"Good," she replied.

Daniel took Alisha in his arms and kissed her everywhere he could. Alisha was elated.

"Daniel, I have never felt like this before."

"Neither have I, and I have had plenty of practice."

"What are we going to do then?" she asked.

"Nothing, we do nothing, nothing has changed, all the minuses are still there."

"I better go – hope you can sleep" Alisha stood up

"Not a chance. I need a whisky."

"I hope that works for you."

Daniel was fighting his emotion.

"Can't see it is helping – you better go. This is getting too serious."

Alisha hung her head and walked to the door, deflated.

"I will walk you home, Alisha."

"Don't bother. I can find my own way," she replied.

She left, slamming the door.

Chapter 3

The next day the talk in the canteen was what a good night the barbecue dance had been. Everyone thoroughly enjoyed it. Daniel didn't comment, as he had too many thoughts going through his head.

"I'll go and check on the herd, and we need to make ready for assessing the cattle before the auction." Dan went to the stables, saddled up, and walked his horse out into the yard. The first person he saw was Alisha. Dan did the usual sexy swing of his leg over his horse and tipped his Stetson at Alisha. She didn't respond. Alisha thought, what a complicated life we lead. I don't know how I am going to cope, but I will. I do not have an alternative.

Three weeks later, Pa mentioned "some good news for Daniel, but not for us."

Alisha's ears popped up.

"Daniels's uncle Tom has died, and he has left his ranch to Dan. He has no other family. Dan is his nephew and used to go and help Tom out quite regularly fencing and walling etc."

Alisha gasped, took a deep breath, and bravely said.

"He will be a big miss to this ranch."

Pa sighed "he certainly will be a miss; I must get him something for his long and excellent service."

Ma said, "I think a cheque would be most helpful, he will have a lot to do on Tom's ranch."

"Yes, a good suggestion."

That afternoon when the men were all busy mucking out and fothering, Alisha made an urgent visit to see Daniel to congratulate him. She approached him, and he put his shovel down and leant against the door.

"I have just heard your good news, Dan, sorry of course, for your uncle Tom."

"Alisha, I need to chat with you. Can I take you out for supper tonight?"

"Fine, say a time."

"Seven pm is good for me. I will call at the house for you. I will book the swan restaurant.

Alisha smiled.

"I will look forward to it, Dan, treat it as a leaving meal."

"No, it's to thank you for assisting with the foaling of Ruby. I do not forget a promise, see you tonight."

Alisha walked away feeling a deep sadness and was fighting with her emotions.

Alisha wanted to make a special effort with her appearance, and I don't know why? I don't have to impress Dan; he will be gone soon. Alisha started to fill up with tears, and she was going to miss him so much.

At seven PM on the dot, there was a knock at the door. On opening, Dan stood there looking dishy but apprehensive.

"You don't mind if I take your daughter out for supper, Norma, I owe her for her veterinary skills, and this is my way of thanking her."

"Not at all, Dan enjoy."

Alisha said.

"You don't have to thank me, but a meal out sounds wonderful – shall we go?" As they left the house, Dan turned to Alisha, "you look amazing. I will be the envy of everyone we see."

"Oh, Dan, your so kind – likewise, you look dashing."

They walked over to the truck, and Dan held the door open for her as she got inside. They headed for the Swan Restaurant, and the conversation was frequent

"Right, I hope we can have nice food and good conversation, Alisha."

"On that subject, can we talk about you leaving? If you need anything, help moving, don't fail to ask."

Dan replied.

"I wonder when I get settled and done repairs to fences could you bring my horse and foal in the horsebox? It would give you a chance to see the place and maybe give me some tips."

Alisha was elated "it would be a pleasure, you just let me know when you are ready to have them, and in the meantime, I will look after them."

Dan sighed deeply. "God, I am going to miss you and your family; you have been like my own family – we must keep in touch always."

Walking into the bar of the Swan, two girls suddenly recognised Daniel.

"Well, if it isn't the king of rodeo, do you remember when you won last year? We both spent the night in bed with you."

"I think your memory of that night is different to mine, yes, I won, went to the bar, got drunk, and some of the boys put me to bed on my own. When I woke up, you two had managed to get into my bed, and you obviously cannot remember me asking you both to leave and not come back. You were not invited, end of the story, now goodnight."

"Sorry, Alisha, not a good start to our night out."

"Let's not let it spoil our meal, Dan."

"Thank you, Alisha, what would you like to drink?"

"I will just have a glass of wine with my meal."

The waiter seated them and handed them menus to browse. Alisha said, "I think I will have something different – urm yes, I will have the seabass."

Dan replied, "I am going to try something that I have never cooked myself, so I will have the lasagne. I am going to have to get used to cooking for myself."

"Dan, tell me your plans for your ranch."

"Well, uncle Tom had been deteriorating for a while. Hence it's been neglected, so my priority will be to fix the place up. I was wondering if you would come and help me check the herd for TB – I will pay you."

"Dan, just let me know when you want me to do it."

"Good, it will mean we get to see each other again." The waiter delivered the meal to the table.

"Would you like another wine, Alisha?

"You're not trying to get me drunk, are you, Dan?"

Dan laughed. "Why would I want to do that? If we ever make love, I want us both to be aware of what we are doing, OK."

Alisha smiled.

"Can't wait."

"Oh, Alisha, do you mean that? Just as well I am going away?" "Come on, let's eat up, and then we can have a sweet." They both ate their meal, both excited and loving every minute.

Alisha thanked Dan for her evening and said, "I really have enjoyed this evening."

"Good, I have loved your company too."

"You will never be short of female company, Dan."

"I am not dwelling on that my priority is going to try and pull this ranch into a profitable venture. I might have to do some rodeo to earn a bit extra – Oh no, I can't do rodeo, what if I get injured? I have the ranch to think of now, so that's a No Go. I will just have to think of something else.

"I am sure you will, Dan."

"Let's take a walk, Alisha, to the river, see if we can see the swans. Dan paid the bill and took Alisha's hand, and they walked to the river. In complete silence. Daniel drove Alisha back to her house on the ranch. He pulled up.

"Thank you, Alisha, for coming with me tonight I have really enjoyed it."

"Me too."

"I am going to seal this evening with a kiss."

Dan pulled Alisha towards him and explored her lips with his. Alisha felt almost faint.

" Glory be Dan, that was mind-blowing, better than the usual peck, goodnight, Mr. West."

"Goodnight, beautiful."

Chapter 4

The day dawned when Daniel had to leave the ranch for his new venture. When he came to the house to say goodbye, there were hugs and tears all around. Dan was part of the family and had worked there since leaving school. It was an exceedingly difficult day for both Dan and Alisha as they tried to fight their emotions and tears.

Alisha's parting words were:

"See you soon, cowboy." It was a sad day.

Uncle Tom's ranch wasn't massive and was about 100 acres. Daniel set to work and hired a local man who he had met at the food store called Roger. Between them, they made their first task to mend the fences. They put in a cattle grid at the entrance and a single gate walkway, and this gave the entrance to the ranch an added design. Next was the woodworking of the ranch buildings and fences. Dan was starting to feel proud of the place, worked hard, and was certainly tired and ready for bed on a night. Dan decided to ring Alisha as it was time for her help. He missed her so much. Work had to come first, though, and Alisha could be a distraction.

Dan asked:

"When would it be convenient to come and test the cattle?"

Alisha suggested "This coming Thursday."

That gave Dan two days to clean the house, change the bedding, and for Roger and himself to make plans for the task of testing the cows. A holding pen was set up, which was channelled into a place to hold a cow where they would be able to do the test and then another channel into the field.

Thursday arrived at 9.00 a.m. Alisha pulled up with the horsebox in tow. After carefully manoeuvring the horsebox into the yard, she got out and looked around. Suddenly she was embraced by Daniel.

"Welcome, babe."

"What a job. I had to find the place. It looks well with the new fences, gate, and cattle grid at the entrance – gosh, you have done a lot of work."

"We sure have, and this young gentleman is Roger, who I couldn't have done it without.

Roger put his hand out to shake her hand. "Hello, Alisha, I have heard so much about you."

"Pleased to meet you, Roger. I am glad Dan has had a helper."

"We make a good team."

"Ma has sent you a few goodies – a roast ham, a pan of soup, and some homemade bread, so I guess when we are busy, it will come in useful."

"Alisha, let us get the horses out of the horse box and see how they like their new home." Roger opened the back door, and Dan went inside, he clapped Ruby on her rump and gave the foal a pat.

"I cannot believe how the colt's grown; you have looked after him very well, Alisha.

"Thank you! It was a pleasure, and it will be lovely to see them in your paddock."

They led the horses out, and it was a proud moment for both Dan and Alisha when they released them, and both animals were cantering around the paddock that Dan now owned.

"Come on, let's grab a coffee and then make a start on the cattle" Dan was eager to get started. Dan put his arm around Alisha's shoulders and guided her into the house.

"No frills Alisha, another project – a challenge at a later date."

"You will probably get a nice young lady to help you with that."

Roger was quick to butt in.

"There have been plenty of ladies making enquiries about him, but he hasn't had the time to go out to meet anyone."

Dan grinned.

"There is only one lady I am interested in, and she is standing next to me now."

"I thought you said you were too old for me?"

"I need to consult you on that point, we will have a few practice rounds soon and see." Dan winked at Alisha, and she could feel herself blushing.

After coffee was taken, Dan, Roger, and Alisha began with testing the castle. A total of 45 were tested before lunch. The three sat down to lunch together and enjoyed the pleasantries that Ma had provided for them. Refreshing homemade soup, fresh bread, and lovely roasted ham. After clearing up, they continued with the testing and worked until 6.30 pm. Daniel had left at 4.00 pm to check on the cattle on the land and returned just as they were finishing.

"A few to finish in the morning, Dan – but coming along nicely," said Roger.

It was nearly time for supper, and Alisha was keen to get cleaned up.

"Would it be all right if I get a shower and change?"

Dan laughed "help yourself and make yourself at home, and you have had a busy long day. Don't think you need an escort this time. I will cut the meat, and we will prepare supper once you're done."

Alisha grinned as she went to freshen up.

"That feels better. There is nothing like warm water to sooth the bones after a busy day," Alisha said as she entered the kitchen.

Dan turned to her:

"Coffee, Tea, or Wine?"

"Coffee for me to start with, we will open a bottle of wine after supper, and we have washed up."

I thought you were a beer man, Dan?"

"I am, but I wasn't going to let you drink a bottle of wine all on your own."

"Thoughtful."

"I am where you are concerned."

Dan and Alisha ate supper and chatted.

"Where do you want me to sleep tonight?" asked Alisha.

"I know where I would like you to sleep, but I am not going to take advantage of you when you have done me such a favour today and cared for the horses. My bed linen has all been changed so I would like you to sleep in my bed and I will sleep on the sofa. I have not got round to furnishing the other room. I have had to prioritise jobs, which I am pleased with the progress, and I have future ideas to update the house."

"Well done, it is looking amazing from what I can see.

Once they had finished eating, they washed up.

"Wine?"

"Oh, not for me, Dan. I am ready to turn in, it's been a busy day, and it's an early start again tomorrow."

"Goodnight, Alisha, and thank you once again. Can I give you a goodnight hug?"

"With pleasure, can I give you a kiss?"

"My pleasure, sweetheart, come here."

Dan wrapped his arms around her and pulled her into his body, and it was a delight but also a hard choice. He wanted to take it further but respected Alisha. They kissed, and Alisha pulled away and headed toward the bathroom.

She undressed for the bed to her panties and t-shirt, did the necessary, and then went into her bedroom for the evening. She slid into bed; she could smell Dan on the linen. Her mind was racing about the events of the day, and she tossed and turned for ages. She decided it was no good and wanted Daniel present beside her. Alisha got out of bed and gingerly entered the living room, fully expecting Daniel to be asleep on the sofa, but no, he was sitting at the table with a glass of scotch whisky.

Alisha startled Dan.

"Alisha, is something the matter?"

"No, I mean yes, I cannot sleep. Knowing you're in the room next door."

"I am going to have a hangover if I drink anymore. God, Alisha, I need you so badly."

"So why deprive each other of some comfort in each other, Dan?"

"You know why. I saw a grey hair tonight when I had a shower which scared me."

"Dan, I love you, and if all your hair was grey, I would still love you."

"That's it, then come here."

Dan picked Alisha up, turned off the lights in the living room and kitchen, and carried her to his bedroom, carefully placing her down in the centre of the bed.

"Do we need these clothes on?" Dan asked, eager to see Alisha's naked body.

"No, it's not cold if you promise to keep me warm."

They kissed passionately.

"I have only got one condom, so we better make the best of it."

"I am sure you will. Just make sure you have more for next week."

They took off what clothes they had on, and each other looked at one another. Alisha couldn't believe that, at last, she was looking into the eyes of the man she had been crazy about since she was a teenager. Daniel was in awe of Alisha's beauty; he was not going to let her go, and he didn't want her all night. At last, they had consummated their union. Daniel knew he would never be with anyone else; he had found the love of his life. He felt content. He told Alisha that there would never be anyone else for him and that she could please do him the honour of marrying him.

Alisha was ecstatic, and a dream had now become a reality. She was tingling from head to toe.

"I will go and see Ma and Pa next week and beg for your hand. Is that ok?"

"Yes, of course, it is. Let me know when you are coming. I would not want to miss seeing you."

"I will give you a ring – ha well, actually I will give you a ring but a diamond ring, but will have one ready for when I have a chat with your Pa. Would you like your Ma there too?"

"Actually, that would be lovely. They have always cared for you."

"Yes, I know that might be a help – right, let's get some sleep, we have got a busy day again tomorrow – night night, darling."

"Goodnight, sweetheart."

Roger arrived before they were up the next morning.

"Come on, where are you all? I will muck out, and you two can make breakfast, so come on."

Dan opened the door looking like he had dressed in a hurry.

"Ok, Roger in here will be out in a minute. I'll just get my boots on."

Alisha arrived looking a bit flushed and nervous.

"Don't look so guilty, Alisha, you are my bride-to-be, and don't you forget it."

"How could I."

Alisha made breakfast, regardless of not having worked in this kitchen before, she managed and put it all in the oven and waited for the boys. They came in and washed their hands. Dan wrapped his arms around Alisha and whispered in her ear.

"Can we tell Roger? I am so excited."

"No, Dan, not until we talk with Pa."

"Oh, Ok, let's eat breakfast."

"Help yourself, I will put it on those plates, and you can make coffee with your old-fashioned coffee pot Dan."

"It's not mine, it's one of Uncle Tom's antiques. If you want one, darling, you can have a new one."

"Come on, you two eat up, I will pour coffee, and then we must go and finish testing the cattle."

"I can hardly believe we had unbelievable success with the first day of TB testing. Not one found to have it," said Roger.

"Come on, let's all wash up and put everything in place because nothing has a place yet."

"Never has had, Uncle Tom just had his own mug, plate, and coffee pot, so this shouldn't take long."

"Right, Roger, bring the first cattle in," said Dan.

"Are you going to give me a hug and a smile this morning?"

"No, to be honest, I am a bit sore and tired. I wasn't on my own last night, remember."

"No, babe, you were not. I loved every moment, sorry if you're feeling a bit naff."

"Oh, it was worth it. Now let's get on the job. We have a lot to do."

"Are you staying again tonight?"

Alisha walked closer to Dan so as not to be heard. "You said you didn't have any more condoms."

"I've got plenty," Roger yelled.

Alisha at once blushed and was embarrassed. She looked at Dan, who was smirking.

"Hell, you must have good hearing, Roger. I will get some later from you."

"Radar ears, my second name, Boss, and yes ok"

The testing wasn't a complete success. Three cattle were assessed as positive and would have to be slaughtered. But that's the only way to eradicate the disease. Everything was tidied up, and Dan and Roger mucked out and fed the stock who were in the sheds.

Alisha went into the house and went for a shower, which was not the most modern, but she felt better, feeling clean, and her hair washed and dried. She then went to the kitchen, peeled some potatoes, and cut them into chips, sliced some of the ham that Ma had sent. There would be enough for a few more days. Oh god, she thought he needed a wife to help him. She felt tears forming in her eyes, hoping it would be her.

After dinner.

"I will help you with your accounts, Dan."

"If I have a tally up and see what I must spend on improving the house, I want to enlarge it, and it needs sprucing up. Both the bathroom and kitchen need some tender loving care. The shower leaves a lot to be desired, something larger, something we can both get in together."

"Sounds like a good plan, Dan. I have some savings from my late grandma that I used some of it on my education, but hopefully, I will get a job and will be able to contribute."

"You can perhaps use some of that on furnishings you would like?"

"I cannot wait." Alisha was so happy.

 "Next job is to go and see Ma and Pa. Keep your fingers crossed, my dear but not your legs."

"Daniel West, what are you like."

"Now, about tomorrow, I must go and see your parents. It's Sunday, will they be at home?"

"They will probably be at church in the afternoon."

"Well, we could join them, and if your Pa gives me his blessing, we could kill two birds with one stone and ask the vicar to marry us as soon as he can."

"You're not messing around, are you?"

“I don’t mess around, Alisha.”

“So, I’ve noticed.”

“I wonder what Pa’s reaction will be?”

“It isn’t as if he doesn’t know me.”

“If he does not approve, would you still marry me?”

“Oh, I don’t know about that.”

“Don’t say that. I would just get Ma to persuade him.”

“Do you think she could?”

“Now you’re making me nervous, Dan.”

“We could always run away and get married in secret.”

“I don’t want to do that, Dan. No, my next plan is to try and get a job, preferably with animals.”

“Yes, that’s what your plan is, I hope you are successful.”

“Now come here. I want to mess around with you, Alisha.”

“Oh no, you won't. I am going to hoover and dust while you deal with jobs you must do. I will change the bed too.”

"On No, Don't, I want to be able to smell your aroma and to imagine you lying beside me in it. Leave the bed until next week, please."

 "Alisha look at that fire, what does it make you think of?"

"Making toast."

"Don't be so daft," Dan laughed. "My thoughts are romantic, you and I curled up together in front of it."

"Have you any wine?"

"Whatever my lady requires."

Dan went ahead with choosing a bottle of red wine and two glasses.

"Oh, Dan, this is lovely, let me just bask in this excellent setting."

"Cheers, my dear, and thank you once again for all you have done."

"It's all part of our partnership."

"God, I love you to bits, think we should make use of Roger's condoms? I wouldn't want them going to waste now."

Dan got up and closed the curtains, and locked the door. He gently removed his clothing, teasing Alisha as he undressed.

"Now come here and let me show you how much I love you, and don't burn yourself getting too near to that lovely fire."

Alisha fell into his arms. After making beautiful love together, the heat brought out the scents of their bodies, an erotic combination of all that was best in good lovemaking. They both slept well that night.

Chapter 5

The next day after doing all the necessary jobs, they each drove their own vehicles. Alisha led the way, Dan was following her, he was incredibly nervous, he hadn't done anything like what he was about to do – asking for permission to marry the love of his life.

At last, they arrived and parked up. Daniel took Alisha's hand, and she grinned and pulled him towards the front door.

Ma was first to see them and looked puzzled as to why they were both together. Both Alisha and Daniel greeted Ma,

"Where is Pa?"

Ma pointed towards the barn.

Daniel walked towards the door to leave. "I must go and see how things are doing. He strode outside and headed for the barn.

Pa looked up "how are you doing, son? How did the testing go?"

"Quite good."

"So, what brings you here today?"

"Well, I hope you have your gun locked away."

"Why." Pa was confused.

"I have got a question to ask you."

"What do you want to know? Is it my best breeding stallion?"

"Well, maybe later, but no, I want to ask you for your blessing and the hand in the marriage of your daughter Alisha. I am in serious love with her. I know I'm a lot older, and I know I have a lot to do to make the ranch viable, but I will give it my best effort."

"Well, son, that's not what I was expecting. Come on into the house, and we will see what Alisha and Ma have to say about this."

Alisha was taking cups out of the cupboard and putting a pot of coffee on the table. She looked up when Pa and Dan entered. Pa summoned Ma to the table.

"We have an important decision to make, Ma."

"What's that?"

"So, Alisha has not said anything?"

"No, just how busy she has been and lots of good comments about how Dan has made such good progress with the ranch."

"Well, I think I need to go and have a look for myself."

Pa walked over to Ma and placed a hand on her shoulder.

"We both need to go for a visit seeing as Daniel has just asked for Alisha's hand in marriage."

Ma threw her hands up in the air, much to her delight.

"Oh, Daniel, you have been like a son to us. Now you will be our son-in-law?"

"Now hold on, Ma, I haven't said yes."

Alisha crossed the room to Dan and put her arms around his waist.

"If you don't give us you're blessing, well, we will elope, Pa."

"Come here, my beautiful daughter, there will be no need to elope. We welcome Dan into our family, don't bother with the coffee; I have a bottle of something stronger in the cupboard. We will drink to this good news."

"I have to drive back home soon, so I better stick with the coffee."

"Norma and I will come to your place and look around, and we can have a drink then to celebrate."

"Are you going to church this afternoon, Ma? Dan and I would like to come to and talk to the reverend about a date to marry us."

"Are you in a hurry?" Ma said.

"Yes, only because we cannot wait to be together.

After lunch, the four of them went off to church. Some of the locals remembered Dan and commented how good it was to see him again. The reverend held out his hand and welcomed them both. They sat through the service and waited until everyone had left. Pa approached Robert the Reverend.

"These two would like to get married in this church, and it appears they want it to be in four weeks. I will see you get a nice donation for the church."

"You don't have to bribe me, Jack." Robert laughed.

"I will be honoured to marry them. Now come into the house, and we can check the diary."

Daniel put his arm around Alisha and said, "that all went quite easy."

"Any requests, Jack? Said Dan.

"Yes, just look after my daughter and quit rodeoing before you break your neck, Dan."

The next few weeks were hectic shopping trips for a dress, shoes all the items that a bride required. Dan even went out and bought a new suit, something he hadn't done in years as his usual dress was jeans.

The wedding day arrived. Roger, the best man, and Daniel arrived at the church in separate cars so that Roger could go back before Dan to attend to chores on the ranch. This gave the wedding couple more time with their guests.

Jack took his daughter's arm as they stood just through the door of the church. The organ struck up with the bridle march. Daniel turned and watched Alisha walk down the aisle towards him. He looked very handsome in his new suit, white shirt, new black boots, and a white carnation in his buttonhole. Dan's eyes glistened as Alisha walked towards him.

Roger, too looked the part, keeping a tight hold of the wedding rings. He was probably as nervous as Dan, dreading giving a speech that was written and safely tucked in his inside pocket. All good stuff to say about the couple who had become good friends to him.

The wedding reception was being held at the Swan – only fitting as it was where they went for their first date, so to speak. A lovely meal was served, and champagne was the tipple. Dan only had a tiny sip, as always conscious of drunk driving laws. Speeches went down very well, the father of the bride spoke well of this beloved daughter and welcomed Dan to the family, saying Dan had always been part of the family and now he was taking a member of his family away with him, which had the congregation laughing as he spoke with his dry sense of humour. Dan and Roger were both word-perfect. Dan brought tears to Alisha's eyes. The wedding cake was cut, photographs taken and then the first dance. Daniel held Alisha tight and whispered in her ear.

"Mrs West, you are my dream come true."

"I can believe after mooning over you for years, you are finally now my handsome husband."

"I cannot wait to get you home, but, as I am only going to do this once, I will savour the day."

The couple were so happy and in love.

Later, when they got home, they found a note pushed through the letterbox from Roger. He thanked the couple for a perfect day. He had checked the stock, and all was fine to get themselves to bed. Good luck, and see you sometime tomorrow.

"It was just a perfect day, Dan."

"Mrs West, now let's have a perfect night." Dan pulled his wife towards the bedroom. Without a doubt, their lovemaking was perfect regardless of them both being tired.

Most married couples would have been going away on honeymoon. They were just so happy to be together, starting their life together.

Chapter 6

The next morning after waking up and making love again, Dan got up to see his stock. Alisha rose and made up a very crumpled bed, had a shower, and decided to give Dan a surprise. She cooked breakfast in just a pinny, no underwear, naked. Her breasts certainly on show. Dan came into the kitchen and stared.

"Alisha, holy Moses, what a sight for my eyes."

"Sit down and eat your breakfast."

"How am I going to eat anything with you looking so inviting?

"Well, lock the door, draw the curtains, and I will put the breakfast in the oven to keep warm." Alisha grinned. "Don't expect this every morning."

"I wouldn't miss this opportunity"

"Bend over the table, Alisha."

Dan unzipped his jean and put his arms around his very sexy-looking wife, and entered her from behind.

"Mind-blowing, Alisha - If I had known this was married life, I would have got married sooner."

"Well, you didn't. I wasn't ready."

"There will never be anyone else for me, I've had sex but never made love before you."

"That was incredible."

"Right, I am going for a shower, then I am just going to pop into town for some shopping."

"I will go and do a stock check; I will take my phone in case you come up with any more ideas."

"I can't think of a better honeymoon. I will get some steaks for supper and a bottle of wine."

"Excellent, come here and let me give you a kiss. Goodbye, and thank you Mrs West, for an unforgettable breakfast.

Alisha wrote out a shopping list and collected her keys and bag, and headed for the local town. First, stop the butchers, she thought. Alisha was smiling to herself and felt so happy. Suddenly, she came across a group of people standing at the side of the road waving their hands in the air, summoning her to stop. They looked very alarmed. She stopped and wound her window down, and asked what was wrong. Incredibly stressed, they told Alisha that their horse had fallen into the river and further up was a waterfall with lots of rocks and that they were afraid for the horse's safety.

"Get in the car we can follow the river to see if we can find the horse. There is a rope under the seat. Can you grab it for me, please?"

Alisha always carried essentials for an emergency, and this obviously was one of those occasions.

They were able to keep the river in their sight and eventually saw the horse. Alisha chose to stop where the road was nearer to the riverbank. Alisha got out of the truck and grabbed the rope.

"I am going to try and put the rope around the horse's head and pull him out of the river."

Alisha dived into the river and swam towards the horse. The water was cold. The horse looked young. Alisha knew from her training that horses could swim and had good lungs. It was a mammoth task, and getting the rope over his head when the horse got near was not easy. She decided to climb on his back, and with a huge struggle, she got the rope over his head. Alisha's biggest worry was how near the waterfall was, and she couldn't risk going over with the horse. Alisha got hold of the horse's mane and started to pull him towards the riverbank. Luckily, they came to an area with a flat stoned edge to the river and made a gallant effort to get the horse to go towards the edge. Alisha remained on the horse's back while it swam to the edge. Once there, she jumped off the horse and pulled with all her might to get the horse onto land. The people from the car ran all the way along the river, they were young and had a mobile phone. They had rung for an ambulance and fire brigade. They grabbed the rope and patted the horse. Alesha lay on the ground, trying to gain her breath and strength. Sirens could be heard approaching.

The firefighters jumped out of their truck and realised the danger was over, and the young people explained to them what had happened.

"Do you realise how near you were from the waterfall; we would have had a different ending to this incident?"

The crew from the ambulance went to Alisha.

"Now then, lady, what's this? We hear you have been a real hero, but you could just as easily be a dead one."

"Oh, don't tell my husband that we only got married yesterday."

The young couple apparently came from the local farm, and their parents arrived and thanked and thanked Alisha for what she had done.

"You must come with us to get dry clothes and warm up."

The ambulance crew checked Alisha's vitals.

"It would be a clever idea to get out of the wet clothes and get a hot drink. Can we have your husband's telephone number, please, so we can tell him your Ok and where to come?" Alisha gave them the number.

The farmer's spouse planned for someone to come for the horse and drive his truck back so he could aid with driving Alisha in her truck to his farm.

On entering the farm. Alisha was shown to the bathroom and given a dressing gown and towels. She showered under a hot shower, put on the dressing gown, and went into the kitchen. She was directed to a chair near the fire, and a mug of warm coffee with a touch of brandy was handed to her.

There was a loud noise of a truck skidding into the yard. The farmer's spouse headed for the door.

"I guess this is a worried husband coming to see what's happened."

She opened the door, and Alisha heard Daniels's voice.

"Where is she?"

"Besides the fire, she is doing ok."

Dan ran to her and knelt on his knees beside her, and wrapped his arms around Alisha.

"Holy Hell, Alisha, are you all right? We only got married yesterday. I could have been a widow today."

The farmer's spouse asked, "would you like a coffee with a drop of brandy in it and your friend?"

Alisha turned to see Roger.

"Don't ever do anything heroic again you nearly give Dan a heart attack."

"Sorry, Darling," she said to Dan.

"Sorry darling, won't cover it, Alisha, you could have gone over that waterfall. I will take a rain check on the coffee thanks. I am going to take Alisha to the hospital and get a better check over."

"No need, Dan – I have been checked over by the ambulance crew."

"There is every need, how much dirty water did you swallow and how much is in your lungs?"

"Thank you, Mr and Mrs Graham. We will come back at a later date and see you and bring your dressing gown back." Dan was adamant he was taking Alisha to the hospital.

Roger agreed to go back to the ranch.

"Did you want some shopping, Alisha?"

"Yes, please – two steaks and a bottle of red wine, please, Roger."

Dan thrust some money into Roger's hand. "See you later, mate."

Alisha went to stand up to leave and thanked everyone for their care.

The couple said, "No, it's us that thanks you. You saved our horse, you took bold action, you were a hero. God bless you, and we hope you will be all right."

"Oh, I am sure I will be."

"I will ring you tonight and tell you how she is doing."

Dan put his arm around Alisha and guided her to the truck. When they got settled in the vehicle, Dan put his arms around her and cried.

"I don't know what I would have done if anything had happened to you."

"Well, it didn't, so please don't hate me."

"Don't ever put yourself at risk again."

"I will try not to; I wouldn't do anything to give you any grief."

"Come on then, let's get me checked out at the hospital."

They parked outside accident and emergency, and Daniel helped Alisha walk into the hospital. A nurse came to them and took particulars, and did all the several check-in procedures. A doctor organised for her to have an ultrasound scan and, after quite a long wait, summoned them to a room to speak with Alisha and Dan. The doctor looked at Alisha seriously.

"Young lady, I am pleased to say there is no damage anywhere, just some extra fluid on your lungs which I would like to give you some antibiotics for to protect from infection from the dirty water you swallowed. You must rest for at least three days. Can you make sure of that Mr West?"

"I definitely will make sure she rests."

"What, 3 whole days – we only got married yesterday."

"So, I heard – complete rest and good luck for your future life."

Dan and Alisha left the hospital.

"Come on, sweetheart, let's get you home."

Chapter 7

Roger was there to welcome them home, set the table, poured soup in a pan, and gave a big hug to Alisha. They sat around the table and chatted about the events that had happened, including their wedding.

Dan held Alisha's hand "right, our hero, bed or a chair by the fire?"

"A chair by the fire and the tv on. Please can I have my book too – I have never got around to reading it."

Roger had been shopping and picked up some lovely steaks. Dan was pleased.

"Roger grab the steaks; I will make supper, and I am going to stay in with you, Alisha, and do some paperwork."

The fire was snug and warm, and Alisha snuggled down into her chair and very soon nodded off. Dan stood and looked at her and couldn't believe how much he loved her and shook his head, thinking about what could have happened and how brave she had been.

The telephone rang, and Dan quickly picked up the phone and answered. He listened to who was on the phone, which turned out to be the press. They had heard about Alisha's heroic rescue and wanted to come and interview her for the newspaper and perhaps the TV.

"Alisha is resting now and not to be disturbed. This is by order of her Dr, so it is not convenient to talk, Goodbye."

Alisha woke up, and Dan made a cup of tea and sat with her putting his arms around her.

"How are you feeling, sweetheart?"

"A bit like I have been on a swim across the lake."

"Rest will be the answer."

Daniel finished supper, and they ate steak and chips with a nice glass of red wine.

Dan turned on the TV, and they watched a day at the races, each choosing a horse in each race. Neither of them would have made a fortune if they had been putting money on.

"Right off to bed we go, and an early night I think," said Dan.

"Ok, Boss, are we making love? I can try."

"No, Alisha, that comes under the category of abstinence. You have to take it easy."

"I am beginning to wish I had let the horse drown."

"Not you, Alisha, not in a month of Sundays would you have allowed that."

"Come on, bed."

The next day after breakfast, Dan put the TV on, and the local television news reported on the rescue of a young horse. They seemed to have all information about Alisha's life history – A rancher's daughter, a student with an extraordinary love of animals, and her recent accomplishment of becoming a veterinary nurse and also her recent marriage.

"Well, well, Mrs West, you are famous."

"Not what I wanted. I just wanted to rescue the poor horse."

"I know, sweetheart."

"Your Ma and Pa and coming to see us tomorrow" "I hope she brings some of her lovely soup."

"I am sure she will. "

The rest of the day, Alisha rested, watched TV, and read a bit of her book. Daniel addressed her every need just like a husband should. Alisha thought I could get used to this. Again, they had an early night, and lovemaking was not on the cards.

"Night, sweetheart, you must rest."

The next day Ma and Pa arrived at 2 pm, loaded with delicious soup and pie. They were appreciative of Dan and how he had cared for Alisha. They showed great concern for her. They were not surprised it had happened, though, as they had always known of her affinity for all animals. Jack took a tour of the ranch and complimented Dan on his improvements to the place. Dan explained to Jack his next mission, which was to enlarge the house, but firstly to make the bunkhouse into somewhere where he and Alisha could live while the alterations were made.

"You could get a caravan for that purpose, Dan."

"Well, Roger, who works for us, needs a place of his own, well, he and his girlfriend. Roger comes from a large family, and him moving out of his parent's home would free up a bit of space. His girlfriend would be the company for Alisha."

"Good idea, then good luck. If I can help you give us a shout."

"That's very kind of you, Jack."

Ma prepared a high tea consisting of the soup and pie which Ma had brought with her. They ate this before Ma and Pa made the journey back to their ranch. Jack and Norma had a lovely visit and left feeling relieved their daughter was fine and being well looked after. Dan and Alisha sat cuddled up in front of the fire and chatted. They retired to bed early.

"Dan"

"Yes, Alisha"

"Would you like me to use my hand for a bit of release for you? She touched his penis."

"Alisha, he laughed – No, I will wait until we can make love together, so snuggle up and go to sleep, babe."

Alisa got up and showered the next day after having a great night's sleep. She showered, and Dan went about jobs on the ranch. Alisha was never left alone for too long as Dan really wanted to make sure she rested.

Alisha knew she had bagged the perfect man and knew this was her last day of rest, and she was keen to get on being the loyal wife and doing the chores of the head of the house.

There was a knock at the door, and Dan answered it to a tall man standing there.

"Hi, sorry to bother you. I am the owner of the veterinary clinic in the next town. We are looking for an assistant and heard about Alisha on the news. I know the press are keen to speak with you. I have come to see you personally to offer you a job in my veterinary surgery. I am in dire need of a helping hand."

"Well, I am looking for employment. Would it be all right to look at your clinic and bring my husband?"

"It certainly would just as soon as you like."

"Well, I am under strict orders from my doctor to have three days' rest, so how about the day after tomorrow."

"That would be great. I will look forward to that. Here is my card with my name and address on it."

"Thank you, this is my husband, Daniel West, he will come with me to look around."

Dan stepped forward and put out his hand.

"Nice to meet you."

Dan took the card from Alisha and studied it.

"Mr Cartland, I presume?"

"That's right, nice to meet you both, and see you all Thursday."

Mr Cartland left.

"What a turn-up for the books, as they say."

"Maybe just what you're looking for, Alisha."

The next day Alisha woke up to find Dan awake, staring at her.

"Morning, Alisha – how are you feeling?"

"Like I need you right now."

"Right off with your nightshirt, and get ready to excite us."

Daniel took hold of his manhood.

"I could have a baby in here if you weren't on the pill."

"Oh, Dan, are you wanting a baby already?"

"Just when you decide."

"It has to be a joint decision when we are both ready, Dan."

"Well, I would love a little girl who looks a lot like you."

"I would love a boy like his handsome father."

"One day, babe, we will just keep getting some practice in."

"Can I take the lead today, Dan? Lie down and let me show you my expertise."

"Continue, Alisha, and I am not going anywhere for a while."

Alisha ran her fingers through the black hairs around Dan's nipple and proceeded to run her hands down his body towards his manhood.

"Alisha, you have had too good of a rest. I think I need you to be gentler with me."

"We are just married and have not had a good start for our love life, my fault."

"We have the rest of our life to make up for it."

Alisha crawled on top of Dan and gently sat down on his penis, gently, but so they were joined together. Dan brushed his lips on her breasts.

"I don't want to ever lose you, Alisha."

"You're never going to lose me until we are old and grey."

A day of housewife duties laid ahead for Alisha, and Daniel caught up on the ranch work. Roger helped.

"Alisha is looking like she is making a good recovery, Dan."

"The rest has done the trick."

Thursday, Dan and Alisha dressed up and got ready to go for a look at the veterinary practice. They informed Roger of their plans, and he wished Alisha luck.

The practice needed some modernising, but Reg Cartland was aware of the work, and he hoped that Alisha could give him advice. Wages were discussed as days of work. Dan kept quiet throughout and took all the offers in mind to discuss with Alisha later. They said their goodbyes to Reg and said that they would be in touch.

"Let's go to the local furniture store whilst in town, Alisha." Dan was aware of how worn the sofa and chairs were, and it would give them an idea of how the money would be needed to replace what had been his uncle Tom's.

"What about dinner?"

"We can go to the fish and chip café and get a takeaway, so come on, and we can make the most of our time in town."

Dan took Alisha's hand and led her to the truck, and they pulled up outside the furniture store. They looked out the window before entering the store. They saw a variety of furniture, Nik Naks, and ornaments. Once inside, they rang the bell for assistance, and a male assistant stepped forward

"Can I help you?"

"Can we take a look at your sofas and chairs, please?"

"No problem, sir, follow me."

They were led to a part of the store where they saw several sitting room suites. Dan and Alisha walked around the furniture and looked for the price tickets and got an idea of how much they would have to have to purchase these items.

"Which one do you prefer, Dan?"

"Probably the brown tweedy one to tone in with the ranch and spice it up with some colourful cushions. Which one do you think? You don't have to agree with me, you will have a better judgement than me."

"No, I think that is a good, wise choice."

"Right, how much is this one?"

The assistant came forward, and they pointed to the brown tweed one.

"We have a sale starting in two weeks which would be 20% off, so that would take it to 380$."

"We don't need it right away, so would you reserve it for us?"

"Come along to the desk, and we can take a deposit and your name and address."

"Wait, I will just have a sit on it first, come on, Alisha, sit with me."

"Do you want to sit in the chairs or sofa? His assistant asked.

"Both, please," they both replied.

Dan was thinking about how little there was in the house suitable, and he needed to decide first to get an architect to go and look at some plans for enlarging the house. It was going to be his plan as soon as possible with Alisha's input of what she would like.

Chapter 8

That night after supper and all jobs were done, they both sat down on the sofa, which was uncomfortably lumpy. Daniel had seen the advert on the noticeboard in town advertising the local rodeo, which stated the prize money, and he made the decision to place an entry. The prize money would pay for a new sofa and chairs. This would leave money in the bank for others items they needed. So, Dan decided to tell Alisha his plans.

Alisha was horrified and certainly not in agreement.

"I would rather sit on a lumpy sofa than end up sitting on my own if you got injured."

The subject got closed, but Dan had made up his mind, and the rodeo was this coming Saturday.

In the meantime, Dan got in touch with a local architect, and Joseph Burns agreed to come out and visit on the first Friday, so things were starting to move.

Alisha was noticeably quiet; she had started work at the clinic and was putting forward a few ideas which Reg was considering. Alisha was worried about Daniel's intentions to enter the local rodeo; she was turning her back on her husband in bed so to let her feelings known. Dan knew this and decided to have another talk with her.

"You know my reputation on the rodeo circuit. I have been a winner for numerous years. The committee wishes I had given somebody else a chance of winning. I must make use of my credentials to make a living."

"You didn't like me taking risks when I rescued that horse, and I don't want you taking risks to fund us a new sofa. So, end of the subject."

"Sorry, Alisha, but I have already entered."

"This is going to be our first fallout."

"No, don't say that, Alisha."

"I already have, so I am going to sleep on the lumpy sofa."

Sure, enough that night, after undressing into her nightshirt Alisha got her pillow off the bed, picked up a blanket from the store cupboard, and went to the sofa. When Daniel entered the bedroom and couldn't find her, he went into the living room and saw her tucked up on the lumpy sofa.

"No way, my precious, we do not sleep separately ever."

Daniel drew off the blanket and picked Alisha up and carried her to their bedroom, and placed her in her usual place in the bed. Dan stripped off his clothes and pulled off Alisha's nightshirt.

"It's your prerogative if you don't want to make love with me, but it's my decision we sleep together, if we fall out, there is no way of making up if we are apart."

"Prerogative is a big word Dan."

"I don't know many big words, Alisha, and I didn't go to college like you. I just went to school and then to work on your Pa's ranch. Started rodeoing, and that was my best shot at making something of myself. That's all I know."

"Oh, Dan, I am sorry for not supporting you."

"What! You have supported me in more ways than I could ever dream of. Now turn around, and let's make up."

"We are not going to sleep or fall out."

Saturday arrived, and Daniel got ready to go to the rodeo. Alisha refused to go with him.

"You know I am not in favour."

"Sorry, sweetheart, give me a hug and wish me good luck. What are you going to do while I am away?"

"Housework, I will get more done with you out of the way hindering me."

Dan left.

In the middle of the afternoon, Alisha received a phone call from the veterinary clinic with a request. A difficult emergency had come in, and Alisha could assist.

"I am on my way."

"What a godsend you are."

Alisha didn't get home until 6.30 pm. Dan's truck was outside, but no sign of him. No light was on in the kitchen. Alisha switched on the light and saw Dan asleep on the lumpy sofa, which was unlike him to sleep during the day and had no light on. Dan roused when he heard Alisha come in.

"Oh no, you've broken something."

"Nothing was broken, just a few bumps and bruises. Where have you been?"

"I have been helping with an emergency operation at work."

"I thought you probably gone home."

"Daniel, I am home. Let me take a look at your bruises."

"My chest"

"Open your shirt."

"I'd rather you didn't see."

"Here, I'll open your shirt."

Alisha gasped.

"Dear lord above, you are black and blue. I hope it was worth it?"

"It was I won."

"Oh, Dan, when did you last take some painkillers?"

"About 2 hours ago."

"I will get you some more and a drink, and then I am going to give you a bath with some muscle relaxer in it."

After taking 2 more painkillers.

"Do you need help to get in the bath? Wait 10 minutes for the pills to work."

"Thank you, Doc."

"Want a hand to take your clothes off?"

"I thought you never asked."

It was a challenge for them both. Daniel was in pain, and Alisha was horrified at the sight of his bruising.

"Do you not think you should have an X-ray?"

"No, I have been here before, a glass of something strong might help later."

"Oh, Dan, what am I going to do with you."

"When the bruising goes down, you can do what you like with me."

After Dan's bath, they ate supper together, and Alisha prepared Dan and Roger's dinner for Monday next. Sunday was tomorrow and a day of rest. Daniel did the minimum he could, with Alisha doing the same.

Chapter 9

The architect showed Daniel and Alisha the plans he had drawn up for the improvements to the house. The drawings were amazing, just what they wished. So, after preparing the groundwork, Dan hired a team of builders to do the work. They worked with skill, and Dan and Roger lent a hand where necessary. Daniel and Alisha moved into the bunkhouse with a minimum of furniture. The table was taken to the work shed, and in his spare time, Dan sanded the table, and with a good waxing, the table was brought back to life. The chairs would take a little longer.

Dan was on the mend after the rodeo and had been working hard on the ranch and with the building works.

Alisha and Dan decided to go out for supper at the local inn just for a change. They met up with a few locals, but later in the evening, a guy approached Alisha. He was extremely intoxicated.

"You are pretty good looking. How would you like to have a drink with me?"

"Not tonight. We are just leaving."

The drunken man was staggering

"Oh, don't say that."

Daniel stood up and put his hand on the chap to stop him from falling into Alisha.

"She doesn't want another drink, thank you."

"Get out of my way. I will try and persuade her."

"Enough, come on, Alisha, we are going."

Keeping Alisha close to his side, they tried to leave. The drunken man tried to delay them.

"Keep away, we are going," yelled Alisha.

The proprietor had spied on what was happening and came from behind the bar.

"Don't mess with this lady. She is the hero who risked her life to save a horse. She doesn't need any hassle from you. Now calm yourself, or you're out."

"I am so sorry. Please forgive me for my manners."

When they got outside, they jumped into Dan's truck.

"You have come famous, Alisha."

"If that's what you get for being famous, I won't bother."

They drove home to the bunkhouse. On arrival poured a glass of wine for Alisha and a glass of whisky for Dan. They both sat and snuggled up on the lumpy, bumpy sofa.

"I cannot wait to get into our house when it's finished and get our new three-piece suite Alisha."

"It won't be long."

Four weeks. And the house was finished. In Dan's spare time, he started on the outside. He built a wall to make a boundary between the house and the paddock. Roger dug borders and laid new turf for the lawns, giving the turf a good watering. Alisha bought shrubs and colourful plants. The pair stood back and looked at the house and garden. They were in awe of their renovated home. Alisha walked to the opposite side of the garden, where a small tree had been planted. She straightened it and looked across at Daniel, who was leaning against the wall, his arms folded across his chest and his legs crossed at his ankles, she smiled at him, and he smiled back. Alisha slowly walked to where Dan was standing.

"Alisha, what were you smiling at?"

"I was just looking at you and thinking what a good-looking cowboy you are."

"Thank you, sweetheart. Let me say to you, you are beautiful on the inside and outside."

"God bless you."

Moving in day was demanding work and exciting. Roger and his girlfriend Judith came and helped. The new sofa and two chairs had been delivered, and Alisha had bought some lovely blue cushions which complimented the new curtains. A large ornate mirror gave the room a touch of class. The restored kitchen table and chairs looked like new ones and were placed in the kitchen. Dan and Roger went into town to get a takeaway for the four of them. Alisha and Judith chatted, and Alisha showed her around the bunkhouse while the guys were out.

"Do what you want Judith to make this place your home? Roger has had quite a lot of experience of making old and tired furniture into something classy."

"I will get him to go round some second-hand shops. It's not a promising idea to get into debt."

Alisha thought she sounded quite sensible and a good match for Roger. The table was set for the guys returning with the food.

"What have you brought us?"

"Pizza and chips and a bottle of coca cola."

"Sit, let's eat."

There was lots of good chat around the table. Daniel stood up and looked around the house.

"I am an incredibly lucky man, a ranch which I will hopefully make profitable in time, a beautiful house, great friends but most of all, the love of my life. Thank you all for your help."

Roger and Judith left.

"Come here, my gorgeous lady."

Daniel and Alisha settled into their new home and loved it. Alisha continued her work at the vets, getting on well with her customers, as well as, always, the animals. Alisha helped with the paperwork on the ranch, which Dan was grateful for.

That year Christmas came and went, with a few parties attended by Alisha and Dan. They decided to throw a New Year's Eve party. Roger and Judith attended and were a good help. As usual, Alisha had a few drinks too many and really enjoyed herself, mixing with the locals. Dan had taken her in his arms and midnight.

"Happy new year sweetheart. I love you so much, and I am so happy."

"I love you too, darling."

After everyone left, Dan scooped Alisha in his arms and took her to bed. He showed her just how much he loved her. The next morning Alisha returned her feelings, and they were late up.

New Year's Day was spent quietly, with a few visitors with New Year greetings. Alisha served up leftovers from the night before and put a roast of beef into the oven for dinner that night. Dan peeled the potatoes, and Alisha did the vegetables, working as a team.

While the meat was roasting, the pair took each other's hands, and they went for a stroll around the ranch. It was a beautiful warm day, and they were commenting on changes ahead. When they returned to the house, they sat down, and each discussed what they thought.

Alisha went first:

"You are a horseman through and through and always have been. I think we should breed more horses to sell at the right time."

"Well, my mind reader, my thoughts exactly. I think your dad would lend us one of his good stallions to make a start. He did think when I went to see him to ask for your hand in marriage that's what I wanted to loan his best stallion."

"We will go and see him together. I am sure he will give us help to start this new venture."

And sure enough, a visit was arranged the following month with Ma and Pa. Roger was informed of their intentions.

They travelled to visit Ma and Pa to discuss loaning their best stallion. All were pleased to see each other. Whilst sitting and discussing their plans, Alisha suddenly jumped up and ran to the bathroom with her hand over her mouth. Dan was concerned and stood up and followed her. He saw her heaving over the toilet basin.

"Have you got an upset stomach?" "Come on, let's get you a glass of water and sit down."

Alisha's Ma looked at her and kept her thoughts to herself. Ma would talk to Alisha when the time was right.

"Would you like a bite to eat, Alisha?" asked Ma.

"No, thank you, Ma," I am going to go outside with Pa and Daniel to look over the stallions."

Pa suggested, "A prize horse with a good breeding record is the best."

Daniel and Alisha were over the moon. They picked a black stallion with a glossy coat. They would be back to pick it up with the horse trailer in the next couple of days. Ruby was in for a treat. Daniel was ecstatic he was now branching out in a new venture and hoped to be a successful horse breeder.

Chapter 10

Driving home, Dan turned to Alisha.

"Are you feeling alright, Alisha?"

"It has been a good day but a long one, and I am ready for my bed."

So, bed was the order of the day when they arrived back at the ranch.

Alisha didn't mention to Daniel that she felt queasy the next morning. She didn't want to alarm him and get his hopes up. Alisha was beginning to suspect the reason.

That night when Daniel took Alisha in his arms, and he fondled her breasts, she whimpered.

"Right Alisha what is going on? I can feel some changes in your body. Is it what I think it is? Oh, I do hope so."

"I am not sure yet. I will get a pregnancy test from the chemist."

"When do you think this may have happened?

"New Year's Eve, I forgot to take my contraception pill, and we sure celebrated the evening with no holds barred."

"It was a night to remember. How do you feel if you were pregnant?"

"It has always been on my agenda to have a baby with my adorable husband, Dan."

"I cannot wait to find out. Can we go to a 24-hour chemist now? Please, Alisha, I would go myself for the kit, but I think people would find it unusual buying a pregnancy test."

"Let's wait until the morning, Dan, please."

"I don't think I will sleep, but if it is positive, then I probably won't sleep for a few weeks."

"Promise we keep this to ourselves, Dan."

"I don't know if I will be able to, Alisha. This is a new experience for us both, if it's positive. Come on, let's have a hot drink and then go to bed. I need a hug, sweetheart."

Morning arrived. Alisha got out of bed and rushed to the bathroom for a few heaves over the sink.

"I don't think there is any need for a pregnancy test," Alisha said.

"You might have food poisoning."

"I don't think so."

"Most babies come unplanned, and this one will be very welcome, Alisha."

"I know, Daniel. I didn't do it on purpose. I am happy about it if only the sickness would stop, but I know it's quite normal in the early stages."

Daniel took Alisha into town and dropped her at the chemist to purchase a pregnancy kit. After that, they went to the bakers and got some pies and then returned home.

Dan sat on the sofa while Alisha went off to the bathroom to perform the deed. She returned to Dan and waited hand in hand with him in anticipation of the pregnancy result. All eyes on the plastic stick.

"Oh, Alisha."

"Oh, Daniel."

The stick had turned blue, and Alisha shouted, "it's positive, Daniel, we are pregnant."

The pair hugged each other.

"Now, I must look after you. You must look after yourself. Promise me, Alisha."

"I will, Daniel."

Dan became a very devoted father-to-be and helped Alisha through her sickness and tiredness. He was so excited to be going to the hospital for their first scan.

On arrival, they were taken to a room where Alisha's blood pressure and weight were taken. She waited with Daniel to be called for her scan. They were led into a room where the midwife welcomed them.

"Lay on the bed, Alisha, please."

The midwife explained the procedure and proceeded to put a cold gel onto Alisha's tummy. Both Alisha and Daniel looked towards the tv monitor. They were both not sure what they were looking at. The midwife went quiet.

"Is everything alright?" asked Daniel.

Alisha squeezed Dan's hand and was worried.

"Have you bought your pram yet?"

"No, not yet. Why is everything ok?" said Alisha.

"Yes, everything is good but are you ready for this?"

They both said in unison, "Yes."

"You are going to need a twin pram. I went quiet because, at first, I could not see the 2nd baby as it was hiding, but now you can see clearly on the monitor 2 heartbeats."

Dan hugged and kissed Alisha.

"Oh, sweetheart, I could not be more delighted."

A shocked Alisha.

"It's alright for you. You don't have to give birth to two babies. I am so nervous."

"My strong and brave wife who is known as the hero."

The midwife cleared Alisha's tummy of the cold gel.

"Now listen, guys, take care and rest as much as possible. Build up your strength to be ready for a wonderful event."

In the coming months, Alisha had to tell work about her news and that she would work until she was too tired to continue. Alisha kept herself well, and the vets made sure she did light duties in the office. Her free time at home was spent getting things ready for the imminent births.

Daniel and Roger continued with their work on the ranch and were happy to find that they had successfully impregnated four horses.

Alisha managed to work for seven months. For Daniel, that wasn't soon enough.

Extra shopping was bought as they now needed items for two babies and purchased some lovely lemon and white baby clothing. Ma was knitting for dear life, and a double pram was purchased.

As the pregnancy progressed to the birth, Alisha became extremely tired and tetchy, which Dan knew was with the strain on her body. Daniel was in the bad books quite often for being overprotective, as Alisha liked to be independent. But he just loved Alisha and her bump and didn't want anything to happen to her.

In the later weeks, Alisha could not sit down and cleaned the house from top to bottom several times. She stocked the freezer with home-cooked meals and packed her bag ready for when it was time to give birth. On occasion, Daniel had got cross with Alisha for doing too much, but this was Alisha's way of getting ready for the arrival of her babies.

Chapter 11

After a long hard day on the ranch, they retired to bed at 10.00 pm. They both snuggled in together the best they could. However, Alisha was uneasy and got up to go to the toilet. Whilst she was in the bathroom, she felt a warm, wet gush.

Alisha went back to the bedroom.

"Daniel, wake up. My waters have broken. We need to go now to the hospital."

Daniel jumped out of bed and dressed himself. He grabbed Alisha's packed suitcase and led Alisha slowly to the truck. Reassuring her as they walked. He rang ahead to the hospital and informed them they were on their way. Daniel drove to the hospital as fast and safely as he could.

On arrival, Daniel eased Alisha into a wheelchair and headed for the maternity wing. The midwife was waiting patiently for them on arrival and led them to a birthing room.

"We are only going to do this once, babe; this is too nerve-racking."

"You should grumble, Dan. I am the one in pain and doing all the work."

"I know you are, sweetheart. I just want to help if I can."

"You can just hold my hand and rub my back when I need you to."

Daniel could see Alisha was in severe pain and felt he was of no use to her.

"Can you pass me the gas and air, Daniel? It's for my use, not yours."

As another contraction came, Alisha applied pressure to Daniels's hand.

"Alisha, you have nearly broken my hand."

"Well, now you know how the pain feels."

The midwife entered.

"Keep doing some nice breathing exercises, Alisha. You're doing well. Would you like an epidural to help with the pain?"

"Not if it's possible to avoid."

On examination, Alisha was 5 cm dilated. The midwife was monitoring her closely. Dan had gone very quiet.

"Are you ok, Daniel?" asked Alisha.

"This is the hardest day of my life."

"But the best," replied the midwife.

Three hours later, the midwife confirmed that the head was crowning. Alisha was exhausted and just wanted it to be over.

"You need to push now, Alisha, when you feel a tightening."

Alisha started to push through the regular contractions. Daniel applied a cool compress to Alisha's forehead to keep her cool.

"Push, Alisha, push. Hold it now, Alisha baby is coming out, and I need to untangle the cord."

As quickly as it was said, a baby shot onto the bed. The midwife quickly did her checks and handed baby number one to Daddy.

"Oh, Alisha, it's a beautiful baby boy."

"Right, Alisha, here comes baby number 2."

Within three minutes, a 2nd baby was born. This was a gorgeous girl. The midwife handed the baby girl to an exhausted but relieved mother.

Daniel lent over Alisha and kissed her, sobbing with joy.

"Thank you, Alisha. We are blessed with adorable twins and just look at them. You did it, Alisha. I am so proud of you."

"My world is complete."

"Our world is complete, Dan."

"Now the hard work begins," they laughed.

Milton Keynes UK
Ingram Content Group UK Ltd.
UKHW040335150224
437844UK00001B/40